MINE

OLIVIA T. TURNER

www.OliviaTTurner.com

Edited by Karen Collins Editing
Cover Design by Olivia T. Turner

COME AND JOIN MY PRIVATE FACEBOOK GROUP!

Become an OTT Lover!

www.facebook.com/groups/OTTLovers

BECOME OBSESSED WITH OTT

Sign up to my mailing list for all the latest OTT news and get a free book that you can't find anywhere else!

OBSESSED
By Olivia T. Turner
A Mailing List Exclusive!

When the rich and powerful CEO Luke Gray looks out his

office window and sees an angel working in the next building, he buys the entire company just to be near her.
But what Zoe is going to find out is that this obsessed and possessive man will not only own her company, but he'll own her too.

Go to www.OliviaTTurner.com to get your free ebook of Obsessed

To my first client Mr. Russell
I would have done a lot more than babysitting for you...

ONE

Carter

"This bottle looks good," Linda says as she looks at the wine menu. "It's aged eighteen years."

"Just how I like it," I mutter under my breath.

"Sorry?" She leans over with a smile and I shake my head. "Nothing."

I drop my eyes back down to the menu, but I'm only seeing one thing and it's not the fifty-six dollar Duck Pâté en Croûte, whatever the fuck that is.

I can't stop thinking about the gorgeous angel in my house right now. Why the fuck am I here when all I've ever wanted is at home?

"I think I'm going to have the Salmon En Papillote," Linda says as she closes her menu.

She looks nervous as she takes a sip of water.

I wonder if she'd be less nervous if she knew that there was no chance of anything happening between us.

It's a first date that my best friend Jacob set me up with. He said I needed to get out more and meet some women.

Well, I met someone tonight, but it's not the woman sitting across the table from me. It's the new babysitter that I left at home.

It had felt like I got struck by lightning when I opened the door and saw her standing there. She was chewing gum and looking up at me with the brightest sparkling blue eyes that I've ever seen.

My heart started hammering in my chest as I stood there, unable to move in her angelic presence. In that moment, I knew I had to have her. I've never wanted anything more.

The sun was at her back, lighting up the golden blonde hair around her head like a halo. Aviator sunglasses were perched on the top of her head like a tiara, making her look like a damn princess. She was staring up at me, just chewing her gum and making those perfect little cherry red lips smack up and down. An image of me sliding my hard cock through them nearly took out my knees. I had to grab onto the doorframe to keep from collapsing.

She looked so damn innocent standing there like she just walked over from any of the houses on the block. My eyes roamed over her body, trying to memorize every detail so I could jerk off to her image at the first chance I got. Her perky little tits made my mouth water as they stood out proudly under her open black leather jacket and white shirt.

She was wearing faded tight jeans that hung low on her young hips. Her knees were popping through big holes, giving me a glimpse of her smooth flawless skin underneath. I wanted to rip them off and see what else she had hidden under there.

My mouth watered when I saw her perfect little feet and sexy toes in flip flops. I don't know why the thought of her barefoot in my house turned me on even more, but it did. Everything about this girl turned me on.

I was actually jealous of Evan. Jealous of a five-year-old.

How could I not be? He got to spend the night with her. Getting hugs, kisses, wrestling. He was the luckiest kid in the world to be able to spend the night in her presence.

"Are you okay?"

Oh, right. My date.

"Huh?"

"You seem very distracted," Linda says. "Are you worried about your son with the new babysitter?"

"Yeah," I say, trying to shake out of my daze. "Sorry, my mind is on the babysitter. I can't seem to stop thinking about her."

"I'm always nervous too when I get a new babysitter for my little Luna." She starts going on about her kid and my mind wanders back to Brooklyn.

Brooklyn's Babysitting Services.

Fuck. I feel like I've downed a twelve pack of energy drinks. I can't sit here anymore.

I would leave right now and head back home, but this is a good friend of Jacob's and I don't want to be a complete ass to her. Plus, my son Evan must be still awake and I need him to be sleeping for what I have planned when I get home.

Brooklyn doesn't know it yet, but she will be mine.

A girl like that needs a man like me to protect her, to watch over her, to pamper her, to own her.

The thought of her at school surrounded by horny boys who have their eyes all over her supple body makes my hands start to shake with anger. The thought of them brushing against her body in the halls, hearing her sweet voice, smelling her intoxicating scent... Fuck, I can't take it.

"Excuse me," I say as I jump up so fast that my chair nearly falls over. Linda's eyes widen in shock as she looks up at me.

"Are you okay?" she asks. "You look really pale."

"I'm just going to use the bathroom."

"Okay," she says as I stomp off to the back of the restaurant.

I've lost my appetite.

My mind is racing as I storm into the men's room. Panic fills every inch of me.

I don't think I'll be able to release it until she's mine. Until her pussy juices have coated my cock. Until my seed is growing in her womb. Until I own her completely.

"Get out," I growl at the guy in the bathroom who's washing his hands. He takes one look at me and then rushes out without drying his hands.

I'm not normally such a hot-headed prick, but this girl has got me on edge.

Brooklyn Bennett.

The babysitter who's going to get a lot more than forty bucks when I get home.

TWO

Brooklyn

"Want to play with my blocks?" Evan asks with the cutest smile on his face.

"Sure!" I say, smiling back at him.

The kid takes off running to his room at the end of the hall and disappears inside.

I take my time walking down the hallway as I look at the pictures on the wall. It's all pictures of Evan from when he's about two years old until now. I notice that there aren't any pictures of him before that as a baby. There also isn't any pictures of his mother anywhere in the house, and believe me, I've looked for them.

The last picture on the wall is the one that stops me in my tracks. Evan is with his father, Carter Ross. I swallow hard as I look at those dark eyes, which seem to be staring back at me. Is there a more beautiful man in the world? I'm not sure. Probably not.

He's holding Evan on his lap and looking at the camera

with a hard stare. Butterflies flutter in my stomach as I examine every detail of this man that has captivated my mind since I walked into his house. He has salt and pepper hair with a light beard that also has the perfect amount of grey. I can't help wondering how it would feel to run my hand up his strong jaw. This is the first time I've been attracted to an older guy—to any guy really—and I find myself intensely curious about him. I want to know everything.

"Are you coming?" Evan asks as he pops his head out of his room with a look of frustration on his face.

There aren't any pictures of Mr. Ross in there to gawk at. I've already checked.

"I coming," I say as I walk over, hoping I get to say those same words to his father.

～

I check on Evan and he is sound asleep. I have the house to myself.

A mischievous grin creeps across my face as I walk down the hall, running my hand in waves along the wall.

I shouldn't, but I'm gonna.

My heart starts beating a little faster as I step into Mr. Ross's bedroom. It's a big master suite with a beautiful ensuite bathroom attached. It smells rich and musky just like him.

It feels naughty being in here and I start to feel a growing heat between my legs. It starts to throb when I look at his big master bed and fantasize what he would do to me in there.

I've never even kissed a boy before and here I am, fantasizing about getting taken by a much older man in every possible way.

I walk on my toes to the lamp beside his bed and turn it on. The room is a warm beige with expensive looking furniture and sleek decorations.

It's not like my mom's small master bedroom with all of the dirty clothes, over-flowing ashtrays, and empty wine bottles scattered everywhere. This master suite looks like it should be on the cover of Rich Sexy Bachelor Magazine.

There's a shirt draped over the chair by the window and before I can stop myself, I'm tiptoeing over and grabbing it. I put it to my nose and inhale deeply, sucking in his rich intoxicating scent. I wonder if he would notice if I stole it.

I don't know what has come over me, but I'm acting like a total psycho. There's just something about the way he was looking at me when he opened the door, like he was a starving man and I was the nourishment he needed to survive. Something about that hungry look in his eyes has flipped a switch inside me. I want him to devour me. I want him to have his fill.

I take one more delicious whiff before putting the shirt back over the chair like I found it. The street is dark and I look both ways for any headlights approaching before I walk over to his nightstand to see what's inside.

My pulse is racing and there's a fluttering in my chest as I open the top drawer. I know it's wrong, but right now all I want is wrong.

There's a box of condoms and an expensive watch inside. I pick up a Magnum and trace my fingertip around the rubber circle, wondering what it would be like to slide one of these over his big cock. Would he do it or would he let me?

The questions are getting me wet and the answers are making my pussy ache.

I've touched myself before but I've never had an orgasm. I could just never bring myself there no matter how hard I tried. But right now I feel like I could explode from just one touch.

Something dark and wicked in me takes over and before I can stop myself, I'm stripping my clothes off and dropping them to the floor. My white cotton panties are soaked with

my desire for Mr. Ross and I picture him sitting in that chair and watching me as I slide them down my legs.

I'm so wet. This is crazy. I'm in a strange man's house, completely naked.

What if he walks in the door and sees me?

That thought makes my clit ache and I slide my hand down to give it some relief.

I'm soaking wet. My fingers come away drenched with sticky syrup.

I rub myself, but it's not enough. I want to be surrounded by his smell. I want to be engulfed in his essence.

The little devil on my shoulder takes over and urges me to slip into his bed. "Imagine what he's going to do when he smells your pussy on his sheets," the devil whispers into my ear.

The angel on the other side is nowhere to be seen. The devil probably bound and gagged her.

I pull back the sheets and slide in between them. They feel so soft and a little bit cold on my hot naked skin.

My eyes close as I lower my head on his pillow, breathing in his arousingly heady scent. I part my legs as my hand slides down my stomach to between my legs. I've never been so turned on. I've never been so wet.

I picture Mr. Ross walking in here and finding his naughty babysitter naked in his bed. I can feel his strong hands on me as he punishes me in the best possible way.

My hand is moving double time as I rub my clit and slide my fingers up and down my soaking wet folds. My back arches off the bed and I have to cover my mouth to keep from screaming as I cum hard all over his sheets.

It takes ages to come down from my orgasm and when I do, my legs are trembling and I can barely breathe.

It was my first orgasm ever and now it's on Mr. Ross's sheets. It belongs to him because it was for him.

My heart is pounding as I sit up and pull back the sheets.

It's a wet mess under there, but I don't regret a thing. Knowing that he's going to be sleeping in this bed with the smell of my juicy cunt in his nose, teasing and taunting him in his dreams makes me smile.

I'm just his babysitter but I want to be so much more.

He calls me to take care of his son, but I want to take care of him.

Maybe after he sees this, he'll let me.

THREE

Carter

I burn through every damn stop sign on the way home. Poor Linda was holding onto the dashboard and saying her prayers as I whipped around the corners like I was Mario fucking Andretti.

"Wow, you like to drive fast," she said as I swerved around a car that was driving too damn slow. I hit the gas and blew past him, anxious and eager to get home.

The desire to see Brooklyn grew with every second that I was stuck in the restaurant until it took on a life on its own, eating and ripping at me with frustration.

"Leave!" it growled at me. "Go claim her before someone else does!"

I spent the entire dinner sweating and white knuckling it as I held onto the arms of my chair while Linda talked about her job and her love of playing the violin.

I just stared at her lips as she talked, pretending to listen,

pretending they were a tenth as interesting as Brooklyn's cherry red lips.

My desire paced within, getting angrier by the second. It huffed with impatience at the slow waiter, at how long it took Linda to finish her damn salad, at France and all of the French people who thought it was a good idea to make dinner have *five* fucking courses!

Each second that ticked by was torture. I would have left if it was anyone else, but Jacob is my best friend and I promised him that I would be a perfect gentleman to Linda.

I'm trying, but it's hard. It's hard to be a perfect gentleman when I'll I can think about is racing home to be a dirty beast with my young babysitter.

The only thing that kept me grounded and sane was knowing that Brooklyn was in my house. That perfect round ass was sitting on my couch. Those sweet cherry red lips were touching my drinking glasses. Those sweet innocent lungs were breathing my air and mixing it with her own.

By the time I paid the bill, my restraint was wearing dangerously thin. I practically grabbed Linda and dragged her to the car.

I think she was expecting a kiss when I dropped her off, but she got a whole lot of nothing. I don't want these lips to touch anything but those cherry red lips waiting for me at home.

My heart is hammering so hard that my doctor would send me to a cardiologist if he heard it as I pull onto my street. I hit the gas and only touch the breaks when I swerve into my parking lot.

My headlights light up the pink bike that's resting on my garage door. It hits me like a punch in the stomach. She's so fucking innocent. I want to smell the bike seat and rub my cock all over it.

I kill the engine and look at my house, knowing she's in there. My dick hardens to the point of pain at the thought and

before I can stop myself, it's out of my pants and I'm jerking off hard.

I think of her bare feet on my couch. I think of her perky tits that were popping out like they wanted to say hi as I stroke my cock even harder. When I think of those ripe cherry lips it's over. Hot spurts of cum shoot everywhere, covering my hand and the steering wheel.

My head drops back and I close my eyes, wondering why I don't feel any release of the tension that's gripping my soul.

I groan as I reach for the tissues and clean up the mess I made.

Once I catch my breath, I take out the keys and head outside. I walk over to her bike and run my finger along the cold pink metal of the frame, wondering if her curves feel as smooth.

"You're a sick fuck," I mutter to myself. "She's too young for you."

But deep down I know that her age won't stop me. I know that *nothing* will stop me.

A rush of adrenaline surges through me as I enter my house and get a whiff of her cotton candy scent. It's silent in the big house and I can feel the heavy thuds of my heart pounding in my ears.

I quietly take off my jacket and shoes and then walk quietly through the house like a predator on the prowl.

My mouth waters when I find her sleeping on my couch. She's laying there so helpless. I could do whatever I want with her, whatever I want *to* her. Her vulnerability makes my cock ache.

I can hear David Attenborough's voice in my head. *The aggressive predator has snuck up on its oblivious prey and is about to sink its deadly fangs into her young supple body.*

She doesn't even know I'm in the room. My cock throbs as I watch her.

I take a knee in front of her and get as close as possible

without touching her. She smells like cotton candy and heaven. I wonder if she tastes as sweet.

The only light in the room is the soft shade of the lamp in the corner. It's not enough. I want spotlights on her to see every crack of her skin, every cell in her body. But it's all I'm given.

She's breathing so softly as she sleeps. Each breath is a treasure that I want to steal. In and out. In and out. It's soothing. Hypnotizing.

I drag my eyes all over her flawless skin from her golden blonde hair that's draped over my couch cushion to her cherry red lips that look so ripe and ready to be plucked.

Her leather jacket is off and my eyes wander down her slender arms, admiring the flawless skin and tiny yellow hairs. Her tits are small but look like they're the perfect size to fit in my mouth. I crane my head and peek down her tank top to see more, but I can't see much with the way the fabric has fallen on her chest.

My eyes continue roaming down, admiring her curves and the way her faded jeans hug her slender hips. I spot tiny blue ink marks on her pocket, probably from bouncing a pen on her jeans as her mind wandered. Wandered where? What does this girl think about? I want to know every thought that's passed through her head.

I wonder if she thinks of other guys and the tightness is back, taking over my body.

Stop, I tell myself. *Don't ruin this perfect moment with thoughts like that.*

I watch her sleep for a long time before the need in me starts to overpower everything else. My fingertips are aching and tingling with the need to touch her soft skin and explore every inch of her young body.

Before I can stop myself, I drag the back of my fingers down her smooth cheek.

She immediately moans and stirs, twisting her body on

the couch as I snap my hand back like I'm a kid who just got his hand caught in the cookie jar.

Her adorable little tits move under her shirt as she stretches her arms out and yawns.

She opens her stunning blue eyes and smiles when she sees me.

"Hi, Mr. Ross."

Her voice is sugary sweet and should be packaged up and sold at Carnivals.

"Hey, little one," I say after swallowing hard. "What were you dreaming of?"

She licks her lips as she watches me.

"You."

My heart starts hammering against my ribs like a sledge-hammer on an anvil.

Fuck, I want her so badly. It takes everything I have to keep my hands by my side.

"How was your date?"

I shake my head as she listens closely. "I won't be seeing her again."

"You were probably too handsome for her anyway," she says with a soft smile. "I could see you with a younger girl."

"How young?"

"Depends. Just old enough maybe."

"How old are you?"

She grins. "Just old enough."

My hard cock pulses and strains against the inside of my pants as I watch her. She's made no effort to get up. She's still lying on the couch like she's ready to be taken.

I lean forward and run my hand along the length of her cheek once again. Only this time, her eyes are not closed. They're locked on me with a hunger that grips my core and urges me on.

She lets out a little moan as I slide my hand down her neck, over her shoulder, and down her sides, grazing the side

of her breast with my wrist as I go. Her legs part when my hand reaches her hip and she lets out a little whimper when my eyes drop to her barely legal teenage pussy.

"You're in my house," I say in a deep gravelly voice. "There's no lying to me when you're in my house."

She swallows hard as she watches me with wide eyes.

"Is your pussy nice and wet for me?"

Her cherry red lips are pressed together but she nods her head yes.

"How wet?" I ask as I slowly trace my hand around her knee and then slide it back up her inner thigh. Her jeans are so rough. I wish I was touching the soft skin underneath instead.

She takes a sharp breath and arches her back off the couch. "So wet," she gasps. "I've been wet all night waiting for you to get home."

Her mouth falls open as my hand travels up her leg. Those pretty cherry red lips are begging to be claimed by a real man.

I lean down to take them as my hand creeps up close. So fucking close…

She lifts her chin to meet my lips when I hear footsteps come racing down the hall.

"Dad!"

Fuck!

Brooklyn jumps up and leaps off the couch as Evan races into the room—wide fucking awake.

"Dad, you're home!" He runs over and gives me a big hug as Brooklyn rushes to the door. She's panting hard and her skin is blushing as red as her lips.

"Wait!" I call out to her, but she quickly opens the door and runs out.

My stomach drops as the door closes.

It's over. The moment is over.

For tonight anyway.

"We played LEGO and watched Paw Patrol and had

pizza," Evan says with his voice racing as he tries to tell me everything.

"You like the new babysitter?" I ask as my eyes glance over to the closed door. Her sweet smell is still all around me, swirling inside my head.

He nods his little head up and down like a jackhammer.

"Good," I say as my heart finally starts to slow. "We'll have her over again. *Real* soon."

He takes my hand and pulls me to his room as he tells me all about his night.

I smile as I watch him. I love the kid.

Even though right now he is the biggest cockblocker on the planet.

FOUR

Carter

C*arter: I need you tonight.*
My body is so tense as I stare at the screen of my cell phone that I feel like my muscles could just shatter at any point.

What is taking her so long?

I hate that she keeps me waiting. I want her at my beck and call. I want access to her whenever I desire. Soon, I'll have it.

A bubble pops up in the right-hand corner of my screen and my breath catches in my throat.

Brooklyn (Babysitter): to watch evan?

It's not to watch Evan. Evan is at my mother's house for the night. I'm all alone.

Carter: Yes.

But she doesn't have to know that.

Brooklyn (Babysitter): another hot date?

Carter: You could say that.

Brooklyn (Babysitter): what time?
Now. I fucking need you right now.
Carter: How soon can you get here?
Brooklyn (Babysitter): 7:00
Fuck. That's in three hours.
Carter: I need you sooner.
Brooklyn (Babysitter): I have soccer practice
Carter: I'll pay triple if you come now.
Brooklyn (Babysitter): I'll see you at 7
Brooklyn (Babysitter): xoxox

I drop my phone on the floor and immediately pull out my hard cock. My chest is tight as I jack off to the image of her sleeping on my couch. I cum fast and hard, but there's no relief. The tension inside me just gets tighter.

Seven o'clock. How many times can I jerk off until then?

I'm pacing my living room like a wild tiger as I glance at the clock every ten seconds. It's 7:02. Where the fuck is she?

An image of me charging onto the soccer field, grabbing her, and throwing her over my shoulder flashes into my head, but then the door rings.

I lunge for the handle and yank the door open, and there she is looking radiant in a pink jean skirt and a white tube top that says *Go Change The World*. With a glimpse, she's already changed mine.

Her lips are the same cherry red, but this time she's not chewing gum as she looks up at me with big blue doe-like eyes. She bites her bottom lip as she flashes her long lashes at me and even though I jacked off at least a dozen times in the past twenty-four hours, I still get rock hard.

"I was starting to think you weren't going to show up," I say as I lean forward, towering over her.

I can feel her heart start beating a little faster, just like mine is.

"You're three minutes late. I'd wait forever for you, but please don't make me."

Her sexy lips part and I nearly pass out when I catch a glimpse of her pink tongue. That mouth should be *mine*. It's driving me mad that I haven't claimed it yet.

"I'm here now," she answers as she walks past me into my house. "At your service."

A whiff of her cotton candy scent hits my nose and I swallow hard, trying to keep myself composed.

I close the door behind her and she does a little jump when I lock it.

"Where's Evan?" she asks as she looks around.

"He's at his grandmother's house."

She slips her hands into her pockets as she gives me an uneasy look.

"What's he doing there, Mr. Ross?"

"Call me, Carter."

She clears her throat and nervously tucks a strand of hair behind her ear as I watch her with ravenous eyes.

"You left before I could pay you last night," I say as I pull out my wallet.

She shakes her head and puts her little hands up. "I don't want to take your money, Mr. Ross."

"Carter. And I insist."

"I'd rather not," she says as I pull out some bills. She places her hand on mine, trying to stop me. "Please. Carter. It was my pleasure. I had fun with Evan."

"And in my bed?"

My eyes narrow on her as her cheeks turn bright red. She takes a step back and drops her eyes to the floor.

"Do you climb into a lot of men's beds?"

I can't breathe while I wait for an answer. I don't want to

know what I'm capable of if she says yes. I'm afraid to find out how far this girl can push me.

She looks so shy and vulnerable as she glances at the exit. She's not leaving here. Especially after what she's put me through.

"I'm sorry."

"For what?"

"For ruining your sheets."

I let out a laugh and she jerks her head back in shock. She thinks she ruined my sheets. After sleeping in her sweet juices all night, I ripped them off the mattress and kept them in a safe place.

"Those were expensive sheets," I say as I stare her down.

I couldn't care less about the fucking sheets, but she looks upset and I can use it to my advantage.

"I know," she says, looking like she's about to cry. "I don't know what got into me. I can repay you for them."

"I don't want your money either."

She looks at me for a moment and then drops her eyes back down to the floor.

"Can I repay you in another way?"

The hair on the back of my neck raises straight up.

"Yes."

She looks back up at me with those innocent blue eyes. "I'll do *anything*," she says as she flashes her long lashes at me.

"Good. Sit on the couch."

She immediately obeys and sits down on the couch. I take my time and walk to the chair facing her.

Her eyes never leave my body as she waits for the next command. I want her to know that this is *my* house and *I'm* in charge. I can make her do whatever I want while she's under my roof.

Her hands are folded on her lap and her back is as straight as a board while she watches me and waits.

I sit back in the chair and cross my legs. "Pull your skirt up."

Her blue eyes widen for a second, but then she pulls her pink jean skirt up to her waist.

"Spread your legs."

My dick throbs as she does. She's wearing a pair of white cotton panties and there's a wet spot over her pussy that's growing bigger in front of my eyes.

The smell of her cunt has been in my nose all day and all of last night. When I went to bed and discovered the little present she had waiting for me, I couldn't believe it. I rubbed the wet spot all over my face and cock. I couldn't go to work today. I couldn't bear to leave it behind.

Every five minutes, I would get up and take another whiff, getting high off the intoxicating scent of her cunt.

I clear my throat to make sure the next words come out firm and clear.

"Show me your pussy."

She hesitates for a moment, but then spreads her legs even wider as her hand drops down. I lean forward in my chair as my mouth moistens.

I can't breathe as she pinches the white cotton fabric with two fingers and peels it off her wet cunt, showing me the prettiest little pink pussy that I've ever seen.

It's glistening wet and looks as ripe as a juicy peach.

"What were you doing to it in my bed?"

She's breathing in short little breaths that make her tits move up and down.

"Touching it."

"How? Show me."

I nearly faint as she slides her slim fingers through her slit. A finger disappears inside her tight hole and she lets out a deep moan as her eyes fall closed. When she drags her finger back out, it's coated in her sticky honey. I watch with bated

breath as she slides it up her folds and rubs her clit in sharp tight circles.

She's getting off in front of me and I watch, mesmerized.

Her free hand starts massaging her tit as her cherry red lips fall open and she cums hard. My cock rages as a rush of clear juices trickles out of her and leaks onto the sofa.

"Goddamn," I mutter under my breath. Could she be more perfect?

She sinks into the couch as her legs close, depriving me of the heavenly view. A long moan rolls up her throat as she sucks on her wet fingers, licking them clean.

Her breaths are quick and ragged like she's just run up a few dozen flights of stairs. "Like that," she says as she looks over at me.

These intense feelings are overwhelming me.

I don't know how to handle them.

She looks so innocent but I know that she can ruin me with one look, one touch. She already has.

"And what were you thinking about?"

She hesitates for a second and then flashes those baby blues at me. "You."

Fuck.

I'm afraid to ask if she's a virgin. Afraid of what I'll do if another guy has seen what she just showed me. I'll take their eyes. I'll take their life.

I grip the armrests of the chair, trying to stay grounded. I feel like I'm going to spiral out of this world. Jealousy was an abstract thought until she arrived on my doorstep. Now it's all too real. It's all too dangerous.

Being with her hurts. It's painful. My cock is aching. My heart feels like it's going to explode.

She's close enough that I can reach out and touch her, but I can't move.

A teenage Medusa who's frozen me with her beauty. I'd

turn to stone if it meant seeing that beautiful pussy one more time.

She quickly gets up with her cheeks reddening. "I should go."

"No!" I reach out to grab her but she's so quick as she races to the door. She's left me so shaken that I can't get up in time to stop her from unlocking the door and rushing out.

And just like that, I'm standing on my porch and watching her bike away down my street with a hard stare on my face.

She won't escape me again.

I'll make damn sure of that.

FIVE

Carter

Last night was pure fucking agony.

After Brooklyn ran out on me, I spiraled into a rage and broke two lamps and my coffee table. I was pissed. Not so much at her, but at the fact that I've never desired anything more. I've never been more tempted, more in need of something in my life.

I was up all night, tossing and turning as I relived the moment over and over again. I couldn't get the image out of my head of her playing with her bare pussy on my couch and the way her face got all twisted up in pleasure as she came.

I still can't.

My breath catches in my throat when I see her run onto the soccer field. Brooklyn is wearing shorts that are way too short to be worn in public and it makes my jaw clench tight.

I want to run out there and cover her up. My muscles are quivering when I spot the football team on the other field watching the girls as they run out and warm up.

They shouldn't be looking at those legs. Those are *my* legs. It's killing me that I haven't tasted what's between them yet.

I focus on controlling my breathing and staying put on the benches. Running over there and dragging her away like a caveman isn't going to do me any good in the long run so I concentrate on staying rooted to the bench. I'm squeezing the metal bench so hard that it burns my knuckles as I watch her bend over while she stretches.

There must be about twenty young girls on the field but I don't take my eyes off of Brooklyn. Even for a second.

I watch the entire practice and get increasingly agitated whenever I see the assistant coach go near her. He looks a bit younger than me and is a little too familiar with the girls for my liking.

His touches linger a little too long and the way he keeps glancing at their asses has me cracking my knuckles in anticipation.

When his hand slides down Brooklyn's arm, I can't take it anymore. I leap off the metal bench and charge over with my hands squeezed into fists.

Brooklyn sees me stomping onto the field and rushes over to meet me.

"What are you doing here?"

I try to step around her, but she blocks my way. I'm staring over her head at the assistant coach who suddenly spots me. I'm giving him a look that would send a grizzly bear fleeing and he turns a deathly pale. He knows what's coming next.

"Please stop," she says as she places her palm on my chest. The anger just rushes out of me with one touch. How can she do that to me so easily? Soothe me with a few soft words and a gentle touch. "Look at me."

I look down at her gorgeous face and swallow hard. Her golden blonde hair is in a ponytail and the flawless skin on

her neck has a sheen of sweat coating it that I just want to lick off and taste.

"Why did you run off again?" I ask her.

Her cheeks start to turn an adorable shade of pink. I love it when she blushes like that.

"I was nervous," she says in a shy voice. "I've never done anything like that before."

My chin raises in hope. "Like what?"

"Like that. Like *anything* like that."

"Are you a virgin?"

Her eyes widen for a second when I say the word and suddenly she's staring at the grass between us. "Yeah." She shifts her weight from foot to foot. "Does that mean you're not going to be interested in me anymore?"

I gently take her chin in my hand and lift it up until her blue eyes are back on mine. "I've never wanted you more. No one has ever tempted me like you have. I've been going nuts the past few days thinking about you every waking second."

Her cherry red lips curl up into a smile. "Really?"

"Yeah. Really. I can't get the image of your pretty pink pussy out of my mind. I've never seen lips so pink before."

She licks her lips as she watches me with excitement in her eyes. "I've been thinking about you too."

My thoughts are filthy. I'm thinking of bending her over right here and claiming her ripe cunt so the whole fucking school can see that she's mine.

When I do take her, it's going to be unprotected with my raw cock. I'm going to slide into that ripe teenage pussy and unload buckets of cum inside her until I'm sure that cunt is nice and bred.

Only then will I be able to breathe again.

"Excuse me!" It's the assistant coach. He's walking over and I was so distracted with the angel in front of me that I didn't notice him approaching. Well, he's got my attention now and he's going to regret it.

My eyes harden as I glare at him.

"You're not allowed to be here."

"You're welcome to try and make me leave."

He recoils in shock and quickly looks me up and down with wide eyes. He gulps and then turns to Brooklyn with a look of indignation on his face.

"Do you know this man?" he asks.

"You don't talk to her," I say in words that come out more like a snarl. "*Ever.*"

He takes a step back and looks like he's about to piss his pants.

"Get out of here or I'll call the police," he says before turning to my girl. "Brooklyn. Let's go."

Brooklyn looks up at me and gives me a soft smile. "It's okay. He's not worth it. Just go home and I'll come see you after. I promise."

I take one last fiery glance at the assistant coach and then exhale long and hard. If I stay here any longer I'll be spending the night in jail instead of in Brooklyn where I belong.

"Alright," I hiss through clenched teeth.

She slides her fingertips down my stomach and blows me a kiss as she jogs back to the bench. Her ass looks so hot in those shorts. I hope she's wearing them when she comes over.

The assistant coach is about to put his hand on her lower back as she jogs past him, but a feral sound rolls out from deep in my chest and his hand drops real quick.

It takes a predator to know one and I know that this guy is no good.

I don't want him anywhere near those sexy legs again.

So I wait.

~

I'm sitting on the benches at a boy's lacrosse game that's going on nearby Brooklyn's soccer practice. The crowd of parents and students are going nuts around me, but I'm not watching any of it. My eyes are fixated on Brooklyn and the assistant coach in the distance.

I breathe a little easier when I watch her get on her bike and ride away. Normally, I'd want to follow her home and make sure that nobody touches her or takes her, but I have other business to attend to.

I slip out of the crowd and start following the assistant coach as he walks over to the school with a huge bag of soccer balls slung over his shoulder.

He disappears into a side door, which leads into the gym. The image of him with his pervy hands on Brooklyn is running through my fuming head on a loop as I catch the door before it closes. I watch him walk across the squeaky floor and then open the large storage room. He starts whistling as he messes around in there.

I'm wondering what else he's touched of my girl as I quietly creep across the gymnasium and sneak into the storage room. The thought of him with his hands on Brooklyn throughout the years, touching her, caressing her, making her uncomfortable causes a flush of heat to barrel through my seething body.

There's one bare lightbulb hanging from the ceiling, swinging side to side like a dead man in a noose. It casts harsh light and shadows on the scuffed up sports equipment all around us.

I quietly close the door and then slide the lock closed. He jumps around like a startled animal when he hears the click.

"Get out of here!" he shouts at me. He's trying to act bold, but I can see through his pathetic veneer. His face is turning as white as his shirt and I can see his hands starting to trem-

ble. He looks around in a panic and then grabs a baseball bat off the rack.

I just stare at him, breathing in and out as he holds it up in warning.

"I saw you touching my property," I say in a low controlled voice.

"What?" His voice is shaky. High-pitched. He's in over his head and he knows it. I'm not an innocent little teenage girl who doesn't know how to fight back. I'm not a helpless little deer in the wild. I'm a wolf like him, only I have bigger teeth.

"Brooklyn. She's *mine*. She belongs to me."

He's breathing fast as he squeezes the bat with sweaty hands. "They're all little sluts. They all like it when I touch them. *Especially* Brooklyn."

A vicious pounding fills my ears as unending surges of adrenaline flow through my veins. My eyes widen and then narrow on him as my hands clench and then unclench at my sides.

I'll kill him for that. I don't care about the consequences. I need to see his blood. I need to see this threat to my girl crushed.

I step forward with my pulse running rampant. I don't care if he has a bat. I don't care if he has a gun, or a whole fucking army in front of him—he's going to pay for *that*.

I swore I'd do anything to protect my Brooklyn and I had creeps and perverts like him in mind when I did.

He swings the bat with a grunt when I approach. I grit my teeth and flex my arm, absorbing the hard blow on my bicep. It's going to hurt later, but I'm in such a rage that I barely feel it.

His eyes widen in panic when I grab the bat and yank it out of his hands. I'm not using this.

I toss it behind me and it bounces on the floor with a clatter. I'm going to use my hands for this guy. We're going to get nice and personal.

I throw a hard jab and my knuckles smash into his mouth. He stumbles backward with a whimper and falls onto the bag of soccer balls. They bounce and roll out everywhere as I leap on him.

"*Who* likes it the best?" I ask, snarling in his face as I grab his collar. "What did you say about my Brooklyn?"

He puts his shaky hands up in front of his bloody face. "Nothing! I'm sorry!"

I yank him closer until he can feel the fury on my breath. "Which hand did you touch her with?"

"I didn't!" His eyes are squeezed shut. He's shaking his head. Sobbing. Weeping. Pathetic.

"Which. Hand?"

I punch him hard in the teeth when he doesn't answer.

"Don't make me ask you again. Which hand?"

He turns his pathetic head away as he lifts up his trembling right hand.

I drop him, letting him fall to the ground as I stand up. I tower over him.

He opens his watery eyes and lets out a sob as he looks up at me.

Now he can know what it feels like to be helpless. To be under someone else's mercy.

Too bad for him, I don't have any mercy.

"Put your hand on the ground." My voice is calm and steady. My heart is beating at a leisurely pace for the first time since I saw Brooklyn. Protecting her is what I was made to do. *This* is what I was made to do.

He slowly puts his trembling hand on the dirty tiled floor and looks up at me with a pleading face. "Please," he whimpers. "Please don't."

"You crossed the line when you went near her," I tell him. "This will make sure you never cross it again."

I stomp on his hand so hard that it crunches. He screams

and wails as he brings his mangled hand to his chest and clutches it.

"You going to touch any girls again?" I ask in a low voice.

"No!" he yells out in a sob.

"You going to touch my Brooklyn?"

He's shaking his head viciously from side to side. "No. Never."

"Good. Because I'll be watching, and next time, I'll cut your fucking hand off."

He chokes back a sob and widens his eyes as I come in nice and close to him.

"And if I see these pervy little eyes looking at what's mine again, I'll take them too. Understand?"

He swallows down a gulp and nods.

"Say it."

"Yes. I understand."

My eyes narrow on him as I stand back up. "Remember," I say as I step back toward the door. "I'll be watching."

He clutches his broken hand and never takes his terrified eyes off me as I slip out the door.

SIX

Brooklyn

Mom is drunk again when I get home from soccer practice. She's passed out on the couch with two bottles of wine on the table. One is empty on its side and the other has a couple of sips left at the bottom. I'm impressed. It's not like mom to leave a bottle of alcohol unfinished.

I open a couple of windows to try and air out the rank smell and then turn the TV off before heading into the kitchen. It's a mess as usual. How can a kitchen with hardly any food in it always be so messy? It doesn't make sense. But then again, not a whole lot makes sense when it comes to my mother.

The fridge has hardly anything in it. Some mustard, a bottle of Vodka that's almost finished, a plate that has something funky growing on it—not much in terms of nourishment.

I'll grab something at the sandwich shop on the corner.

The man who works there is so sweet and he usually gives me some grilled veggies on the side for free. He knows my mother and he's never said anything, but I think he feels bad about my situation.

My room is off the kitchen in our small little place. It's basically the small cot I've had my entire life and a night table. What little clothes I have are kept under the bed in bins.

I take a quick shower and get ready for my night with Carter. I put my cherry red lipstick on that I know he likes and a white summer dress with a pattern of yellow flowers on it that I got last year for my cousin's wedding. I bought it secondhand and it's a little bit worn through, but hopefully, Carter will like it.

My stomach growls by the time I'm ready and I open my night table to get my stash of babysitting money that I've collected. I keep having to dip into it to buy food and last month I had to pay the landlord when my mother came up short so I only have a little over a hundred dollars. I just need enough for a sandwich.

"No…" My stomach drops when I open my pencil case and see that it's empty. She took everything. I should have known, there were about a dozen new bottles on the counter. She had to find that money somewhere.

I storm out of my room and glance at the calendar on the fridge as I make my way to the couch.

"Mom!" I yell as I shake her hard. She just groans. "Mom! Wake up!"

It takes a few minutes but I finally get her conscious. She winces as she sits up and it's not ten seconds before she grabs the almost empty bottle of wine and downs the rest of it.

"Shouldn't you be at work?" I ask as I stare at her with my arms crossed over my chest.

She works part-time in a diner as a waitress. It's a miracle she's still managed to hold onto the job this long.

"No," she says before taking another swig of the empty bottle, trying to get every last drop. "It's Wednesday."

"It's *Friday*," I correct. "You're supposed to be working."

"Shit." She sighs as she reaches for her pack of cigarettes and pulls one out. I watch as she lights it and takes a long drag. "I'll just tell them you got in a car accident or something."

"Great," I mutter under my breath. "Any change from my babysitting money that you spent?"

She pulls another long drag on her smoke as she stares at the TV that's turned off. "I'll pay you back next time."

"Next time what? You ditch work?"

Her bloodshot eyes narrow on me. "If I knew you were going to grow up to be a snotty little bitch I would have taken care of you like your father begged me to."

"Nice mom," I say as I shake my head. "Enjoy your bottles that I paid for. It should be enough to last you the night."

"Yeah, yeah, miss perfect," she mutters as she turns away and sucks on her cigarette.

I grab my purse and leave.

"Where are you going?" she calls out as I open the door.

"Babysitting. At least one of us has to work."

She says something nasty, but I don't stop to listen as I shut the door and hurry over to my bike. I get on and start pedaling fast down the street. The warm breeze hits my face as the summer evening sun warms my shoulders. I feel better with every inch that I get away from that house.

I'm sick of living like this. Sick of living with her.

I push my mother out of my mind and focus on Carter. A smile creeps across my face when I remember my soccer practice. I couldn't believe he came to see me. The other girls teased me after and some even said that he was too old for me, but they don't what he's like to be around. If they only go for boys their own age, then they don't know what they're missing.

It's exciting and thrilling to be around him. It feels dangerous and naughty. It's like being around a tiger. It's fun to pet him, but in the back of your mind, you know that he could just pounce at any second and devour you whole.

I'm intrigued by him. Lately, he's been on my mind non-stop. My feelings are growing beyond lust, but I realize that I don't really know anything about him. He could have a girl-friend or even be married. I want him more than anything, but I won't be a side dish.

My mother was a side dish and it broke her. For a decade, my worthless father strung her along while he took care of his real family in Chicago.

Three beautiful kids and a pretty little wife. They were the good family. The good family got him on holidays and on weekend mornings when he made pancakes into funny little shapes with real maple syrup poured all over them. He took the good family on road trips and vacations to see Europe when all I got to see was their happy pictures. The five of them smiling in front of the Eiffel Tower, smiling in front of the Parthenon, smiling as they held up the Leaning Tower of Pisa. Always smiling. Smiling, smiling, smiling.

He was always proud to show off his good family. Us? Not so much.

We were the bad family. The trash he kept hidden.

We got him when he told his good family that he had to get away for business. Two days one month. Three days another. Some months nothing. Most months nothing. Always mid-week. Always awkward.

His oldest kid is older than me so I always figured that he was already married when he met my mother. A one night stand that went horribly wrong.

I was the thing that went horribly wrong.

My mom always drank, but it got really bad when the wife—the good wife—found out about us and he stopped coming around.

Him and his perfect smiling family can go to hell as far as I'm concerned.

I'll never be like my mother. I'll never be the side dish.

If I can't have Carter all to myself, then I'll end it. Whatever 'it' is.

I ride through my shitty part of town and finally get into the nice part where there are big green trees that tower over the street like they're watching over and protecting the residents below.

I pass one expensive car and big house after another, wishing that one day I could live like this. I know just who I would like to share it with.

Carter is sitting on the porch when I pull into his driveway. Butterflies flutter into my stomach as his dark eyes lock onto me.

He's so sexy. The way he watches me. The way his breath picks up every time he looks at me as if he's seeing the most beautiful girl in the world. I feel stunning and irresistible whenever his eyes are on me and it turns me on every time.

I didn't even think a man like him would look at me in that way, but Carter can't seem to look away. He stands up and my stomach does a little flip as he walks down the steps to greet me.

My body starts to react in a strong way as I look him up and down. He's wearing a fitted blue collared shirt that's open at the top with the sleeves rolled up his thick forearms and a gray vest on top. His designer jeans look expensive and worth every penny with the way they form around his muscular thighs.

I feel an intense animal attraction to him as he grabs a hold of my bike and towers over me. I can't explain it.

"Come inside," he says in a voice so deep that it makes my heart start to pound.

"Is Evan here?"

"No. It's just the two of us."

He reaches for me, but I step back. "Where's his mom?"

I wince as he looks at me funny. "The fuck if I know."

I want to jump in his arms, but I stand my ground. I have to know the truth first. "Are you married?"

He laughs. "To Evan's mom?"

"Yeah."

His eyes soften as he looks down at me. "I don't even know her name, Brooklyn. I met her six years ago on vacation. We were both drunk. There was a closet."

My eyes close as a sharp pain hits my heart. I don't like thinking of him with anyone like that. It hurts too much.

"It was so fast," he says, shaking his head as he looks at me. "I didn't see her again until three years ago."

"What happened then?" Not another closet incident I hope.

"She showed up at my doorstep with a two-year-old. She told me his name was Evan and that he was mine. I didn't even recognize her so I went inside to call the police. By the time I got to my phone, I heard her tires squealing down the street and a two-year-old crying on my doorstep."

"So you're not married? No girlfriend?"

"I've been too busy with work and with Evan to think about women or sex," he says. "Until I met you. Now it's all I can think about."

The tension in my body floats away and I can't seem to wipe this goofy grin off my face.

"Shit, Brooklyn," he says as he takes my hand in his. "Were you worried that you weren't the only one?"

I swallow hard as my cheeks redden in embarrassment. "A little bit."

He suddenly grabs me and brings his mouth down hard on mine, stealing my breath as he claims my mouth in a deep dominant kiss. He thrusts his tongue into my mouth and it's so hot and sexy that it makes my toes curl in my flip flops.

When he pulls away, he's staring at me with such intensity that it makes my pussy tingle. I guess that answers that.

"You're the *only* one for me," he says. "And if you stop running away from me, princess, I'll show you just how much you're mine."

His hand slides down to my wrist and he grabs me in a firm hold. I'm getting wetter and wetter as he pulls me inside.

When the door closes, he pulls a piece of pink ribbon from his pocket and ties it tight around my wrist.

"What's this for?" I ask when he holds onto the other end like he's never going to let go.

"You hopped away from me twice already, little bunny," he says in a growly voice. "And the big bad wolf is making sure you won't escape a third time."

A fluttering fills my chest as he pulls me back to the couch and sits me down. He holds onto the ribbon and I'm trapped, but there's no place I'd rather be.

"Now, little bunny. Where were we?"

SEVEN

Carter

I don't know how many times the pink ribbon is wrapped around my hand, but it's enough that she's not going anywhere. Not this time.

She's in the same spot on the sofa that she was last time. Her smooth legs are spread over the wet spot that I kept marked on my couch.

"Pull your dress up and open your legs." My words come out sharp and harsh. I should be gentle and romantic with her considering this is her first time, but the frustration and need in me has boiled over and I can't tone it back.

Brooklyn looks up at me with a hint of excitement in her sparkling blue eyes as she spreads her legs apart. My sharp commands seem to turn her on even more. Well, if that's the case, then we're going to get along just fine.

My breath quickens and I swallow hard as she grabs her thin dress and slowly drags it up her thighs. I'm worried I'm going to pass out as I watch the fabric rise one inch at a time.

"I can't wait to get you in my bed. That wet spot you left me will seem like a puddle compared to the ocean we'll make."

She tugs the last of her dress up and I groan when she shows me her panties that are getting soaked through by her wet pussy underneath.

My cock is rock hard and aching. I'm holding onto the ribbon that's tied to her wrist real tight. She's not running away and leaving me with my cock in my hand this time. This time I'm getting a taste. This time I'm taking *everything*.

"If I let you go would you run away?"

She's breathing heavily as she looks up at me with a lusty haze over her eyes. She looks like she wants this as bad as I do.

"No," she moans. "I want to be yours."

"You are mine. Haven't I made that clear?"

"Yes, you have," she says with a breathy laugh. "You've *definitely* made that clear, but I want you to *make* me yours."

"That's coming. Whether you're ready for it or not."

She licks her cherry red lips and the wet spot on her pussy gets a little bigger. Fucking hell. She looks so young and innocent. How can a teenage girl be so damn tempting?

"When did you turn eighteen?"

Her big blue eyes narrow in confusion as she looks up at me. "About a month ago. Why?"

A month ago. Fuck. She's barely legal.

I don't know what I would have done if she walked into my house a few months ago. The same thing probably. Would I have still trapped her and fucked her little pussy raw and unprotected like I plan to do now?

Would I have cared that she wasn't legal? Would it have stopped me?

I roll my shoulders back as I look down at her, knowing the truth. Nothing would have stopped me. Not now and not a few months ago.

A couple of laws would never change the fact that this girl is mine.

"If your pussy gets any wetter, it's going to leak all over my couch. Let me see how wet you are."

She lets out a throaty moan and her eyes drift closed as she reaches down and slides her finger over the wet spot. I'm transfixed as I stare at it. Her pink pussy is barely visible through the thin wet cotton.

"Show me."

Her finger lingers, rubbing little circles over the wet material.

"I want you to do it."

She leans back on the sofa with her legs spread open, looking up at me with a challenging look in her eyes. When she brings her fingers to her mouth and sucks them, my legs give out and I drop to my knees in front of her.

The delicious scent of her sweet honey fills my nose and sends me spiraling. I can't get enough of that smell and soon it's going to be on me every day. On my chin, on my lips, on my fingers, on my cock. Not a morning will pass that I won't be buried between her legs, soaking up her sticky nectar.

She'll live with me now. She'll wake up in my bed with my cock buried deep inside her.

I'll send her off to school coated in my cum and all of the boys will know to stay away. She'll be walking differently after I get done with her and they'll see that a real man has claimed her young ripe body. And if they don't get the hint and a boy dares to touch her in any way, then I'll go down to the school and deal with them in the same way that I dealt with her coach.

They'll pay a man's price if they touch what's mine.

Her whole body shivers as I reach down and grab the hem of her panties with my thumb and index finger. The white cotton is soaked through. I knew this pussy was ripe and juicy.

"Let's see these pink lips once again."

She lets out a deep moan as I peel the fabric to the side, revealing her soaking wet bare cunt. It's even more pink than I remembered. It's fucking beautiful and it makes my heart hurt to look at it.

"Do you like it?" she asks with cheeks as pink as her spread cunt.

"Oh, Brooklyn," I moan. "I love it. It's like peeking into heaven."

She shivers and opens her sexy mouth as I reach in and slide my fingers up her folds. She's so soft. Exactly like an untouched pussy should feel like.

I place my hand on her little blonde pubes and rub her engorged clit that's peeking through her glistening folds. This gets her moaning up a storm and she spreads her legs even wider.

"Listen to what I'm going to do to you, princess," I say as I rub little circles on her clit. "I'm going to taste this pussy and you're going to cum on my mouth."

She licks her lips as she nods her head up and down. She looks like she's already ready to cum now.

"Then, once I've licked every inch of you. I'm going to take out my hard cock and slide it in raw. That means no condoms. No protection."

She starts massaging her little tits as I drag my fingers back down to her tight hole. I test it with the tip of my finger and groan at the tightness of it.

"Won't I get pregnant?" she says in moans as she starts to roll her hips on my hand.

"I want you to get pregnant," I say as I go back to rubbing her clit. "I'm going to fuck you in your unprotected pussy and shoot my load so hard that it coats your virgin womb. The thought of you carrying my kid makes me so fucking hard."

I can feel my cock aching in my pants. It's dripping cum everywhere.

With my free hand, I unbuckle my pants and pull it out. Her greedy eyes go straight to it and she lets out a whimper when she sees how big it is.

"Do you want this cock?" I ask as I start to jack off with long powerful strokes.

She bites her bottom lip and nods her head.

"Say it."

"Yes," she moans. "I want you to fucking me with your cock."

"Bare and unprotected?"

"However you want." She's practically cumming on my hand, she's so close. My fingers and palm are coated in her sticky juices as she moans uncontrollably. "Stick a baby in me. *Breed* me. I'm yours completely."

"Good girl."

I grab her panties with my hand and rip them right off. There's nothing covering her sweetness now and her pussy is on full display, begging to be claimed.

She lets out a low feral cry as I lick her cunt with one long hot lap of my tongue. Has anything ever tasted so sweet?

Her fingers slide through my hair and she grabs a hold of it as I fucking devour her. My tongue slides everywhere—inside her tight hole, up her pink folds, around and over her clit. She squeezes my head with her thighs and lifts her ass off the couch as I bury my tongue in deep.

The more I eat her out, the harder my dick gets. It's dripping cum all over my pants, making a sticky mess. My balls are so tight from all the cum my body wants to pump inside her.

She reaches down and grabs my cock, stroking me as I flick her clit with my tongue.

"In a minute, princess," I say as I grab her wrist and pull her hand away. Her hand feels so fucking good on me, but I

want to please her first. I want her to enjoy this so she'll never want to leave. "Lay back down and relax. Enjoy this. You kept your cherry safe for me and it's time for me to repay you for that."

She lets out a moan as I trace her tight entrance with my tongue. Her hips are grinding against my face with every lick of my tongue and touch of my lips.

I look up from her cunt and see her eyes squeezed shut and her cherry red lips wide open. She's massaging her tits, but they're still in her dress so I reach up and yank it down, freeing them. Her nipples are hard and as pink as her pussy.

I want to her to cum on my mouth before I bury my cock inside her. Not only for the sweet taste, but it will help loosen her up because this tight pussy is anything but loose.

My big dick is going to hurt going in, but only the first time. Once I stretch her out a few times, I'll be able to ride her whenever I want and we'll both feel nothing but pure bliss.

I slide my hands under her soft ass cheeks and lift her up as I pull her against my hungry mouth.

"Oh, Carter," she moans desperately as her body starts to buck. I don't stop for a second. I just keep licking and sucking her relentlessly as her legs shake and her pussy clenches.

She cums hard on my mouth, crying out and twisting in my arms as I press her cunt to my face. A rush of warm delicious juice surges onto my mouth and trickles down my chin as I lap up every drop that I can get.

Her legs are trembling around me as she gasps for air.

"See how hard you came, princess?" I start rubbing her clit softly as she comes down from the high of her orgasm. "That's because this ripe pussy is ready to be plucked. It needs my cock buried in it. It needs to be bred."

I continue rubbing her clit as I move up and kiss her tits. Her nipples are so hard and I take one in my mouth at a time, sucking and tracing my tongue around them as she arches her back to give me more.

"I'm bringing you into my room," I say as I tug on the ribbon that's tied around her wrist. "You're going to take off your dress, lay on my bed, grab the back of your knees and pull your legs apart."

She moans as she runs her hands through my hair and moves my mouth to her other breast.

"It's time to plant my thick heavy load inside you and get your young virgin womb pregnant. We're going to make a new wet spot on the sheets with your busted cherry. Together."

I can feel her heart beating fast and hard through her chest. "I'm ready," she says in a husky voice.

"Good." I stand up and tug the pink ribbon, pulling her up. "Because you're *mine* now."

EIGHT

Carter

She whimpers and moans, but doesn't resist as I pull her into my master bedroom.

"I'm still not going to let you go, princess," I say as I tie the pink ribbon to my king-sized bed. "Not until I've marked your pussy with my cum. You ran out on me twice, and I can't risk it again."

She's still breathing heavily from her orgasm and she's got that lust-filled look on her face as she watches me tie her to the bed frame.

"You're in my house and that means I'm in charge. And once I sink into that pussy, I'll be in charge of you. I'll take care of you and give you whatever you need. But you'll be mine. I'll possess you in every way."

I trace her soft slender jaw with the back of my hand and then take her chin in my grasp. She lets out a little moan as I touch her bottom lip with my thumb and gently pull it down to see her straight white teeth.

"Are you ready to come live with me?"

Her sexy blue eyes lock onto mine and she nods.

"Are you ready to have my baby?"

She nods again.

"I know I can be a little obsessed."

"A little?" she whispers with a sly grin.

I laugh. "I know I can be a little crazy at times, but it's for your own good. You must know that everything I do is for your own good."

She kisses the tip of my thumb and moans. "I know."

"Good. Now take off your dress. Take off everything."

I step back and watch with my dick aching as she wiggles her young body out of the white and yellow summer dress. She looks ravishing in it, but it's old and frayed. She deserves the best of everything and starting tomorrow, once I can drag myself away from her cunt, I'll get her the best. Clothes, a car, computer, whatever she wants, it's hers.

Fresh drops of cream drip out of my cock when she slides the dress down her perky little tits. They're small now but they'll be nice and full once my baby is inside her. I can't wait to see her belly rounded and her breasts overflowing with milk. It will be for the baby, but I'll take the first sip.

When the ribbon that's tied to her wrist stops her strap from descending, I walk over and grab it. With a quick yank, I rip it in two.

The dress falls all the way down to her ankles, and she steps out of it completely naked. My eyes feel like they're going to melt as they roam all over her young teenage body.

Her cunt is still dripping and the soft skin on her inner thighs is sticky and wet. This girl has waited long enough.

"On the bed. Legs up."

She lies down on the comforter, grabs her knees, and pulls them up just like I ordered her to. Her sleek pink pussy looks riper than ever as she spreads it apart. Her ass lifts in the air and I can see her tight little pink asshole tempting me.

nails into my arms as her pussy gets used to the thick size of my cock.

I move down to her tits and suck on her nipples as I picture how good they're going to taste when she has milky cream leaking from them.

When she starts moaning and rolling her hips, I know that she's ready for more. I slowly drag my cock out and then start giving her harder, longer thrusts. She grips my arms tight, but urges me on with those sexy blue eyes.

It's a wet mess between us full of juices and virginity and cum that won't stop leaking out of my hard cock.

"It feels so good," she moans into my neck. "Your cock is so fucking big."

I grab her soft thigh and plow into her with a few hard thrusts that have her crying out loud. I'm already ready to cum, but I want this perfect moment to last so I pull out of her. It's sudden and unexpected and she lets out a cry of agony.

"Turn around. Put that sweet ass in the air for me."

She jumps up so fast and plants herself on her hands and knees on the bed. Her gorgeous ass is thrust in the air, begging to be taken.

I lean down as I stroke my wet cock and give her pink asshole a few soft licks. She moans as I drag my tongue down to her cunt and make a mess on my face.

"Your tongue feels so good," she moans. "But I need that big dick back in me."

I laugh as I grab her ass and press the tip of my cock to her tight hole. "You're already addicted to my cock are you? After only one time."

"I'm addicted to you," she says as she grabs a fistful of sheets. "And your cock. *Especially* your cock."

I chuckle as I slide back inside her tight warmth. She's giving me a beautiful view of her young teenage asshole between her two round cheeks. Her gorgeous golden blonde

hair is draped on her back as she looks back at me with lust-filled eyes.

I grab a cheek in each hand and fuck her hard. She lets out deep cries and moans with each powerful thrust and I'm groaning behind her like a feral animal in heat.

"Cum in me," she begs. "Cum in my pussy and *breed* me."

My grip tightens on her ass as my whole body clenches. I give her one last hard thrust and root my cock in her as I cum hard. Warm cream fills her insides and coats every inch of her teenage cunt. It drips out between us and trickles down my balls and onto the back of her thighs.

I scoop my arm around her and lift her up until she's on her knees with her back pressed against my chest. My arm wraps around her and my big hand swallows her tits as my other hand slides down her flat stomach.

I touch her engorged clit and rub it in tight circles as her pussy sucks up every last drop of cum that's still oozing out of me.

Her body reacts in a strong way and she starts to shake and convulse as I hold her up with my arm. She opens her mouth and lets out a scream so loud that the neighbors must hear as her pussy clenches and cums on my cock.

I feel a rush of wet heat on my dick and it pours out between us, running down our legs and making a big wet spot on the sheets.

I hold her tight as her orgasm rips through her in the most devastating way. Her body goes limp and my arm is the only thing holding her up.

Her eyes are closed and she lets out a moan as I kiss the back of her neck and then lower her onto the sheets.

I'm not ready to come out of her tight pussy yet, so I lie down beside her as I enjoy the warm tight squeeze on my shaft.

I dig my nose into her hair, inhaling the sweet cotton

candy scent of my princess. She's mine now and I get to keep her. I couldn't be happier.

When her breathing returns to normal and her legs stop shaking, I slide my cock out of her and untie the ribbon from her wrist, freeing her.

But she's not free. Not anymore.

"You can never leave me now. My seed is growing inside you."

"I would never leave," she says as she slides two fingers into her tight hole. They're a sticky white when she pulls them out. I let out a groan when I watch her put them between her cherry red lips and suck them clean. "Not when you fuck me like that."

"It's not just sex with me." My pulse is racing with nerves as I open up to her, raw and vulnerable. "I love you, Brooklyn. You're the girl for me and I love you with all of my heart."

Those cherry red lips curl up into a big smile as she gets up and jumps into my arms. She kisses my lips as she grinds her spread cunt against my cock that's getting harder by the second.

"I love you too, Carter. We're going to be so happy together."

I reach down and slide my hard cock into her wet pussy as I hold her up. She moans as I thrust all the way in.

"We're already so happy, princess. And once our baby comes, we'll be even happier."

EPILOGUE

Brooklyn

A month later

"Be quiet," I whisper as I hold him tight. "The big bad wolf will get us."

Evan tries to stay quiet but he squeals in excitement. We're hiding in the closet and playing hide and go seek with Carter.

"He's coming," Evan whispers as we hear big heavy footsteps come thumping down the hall. It's dark in the closet, but I know every inch of it intimately. I'm ashamed to admit that I've spent more than a few hours in here, marveling at all of the beautiful designer clothes that Carter has bought me. Anything I want, he gets for me. I never ask him for anything, but he keeps buying me stuff. In only a month he's filled this closet full of clothes, shoes, coats, purses, and jewelry. I've

always been forced to chose from the meager choices at the thrift shop, so this feels very, very nice.

Evan giggles nervously as Carter thumps into the room, making a loud show as he looks around. He's a ball of energy in my arms as we wait to get caught. I love this kid.

And I love his dad.

It's only been a month since I left my mom's house and moved in, but it's felt like I've been here forever. We all get along so well and I'm in love with my new family.

But it's not just the three of us. I'm one month pregnant as well. Carter put his baby in me just like he promised he would. I can't wait to feel it growing inside me and to see how Carter looks at me when all of my curves fill out.

He's already set up the baby's room and it's Pinterest worthy. It looks adorable.

I love that we're his first choice. We're not some shameful secret kept on the side. We're the real deal. His everything. It feels good to be wanted for once.

Evan grips my arm with his little hands as Carter approaches. My heart pounds. Not out of nerves or fear, but from anticipation to see him. Every time I'm away from him, even for a few minutes, it's like a big sense of relief comes over me when I see those dark eyes again.

This house is amazing. In my mom's tiny house there might be two, maybe three, spots to hide. In this luxurious place, we can play hide and go seek for weeks and never choose the same spot twice. The fridge is always overflowing with food and the best part is that Carter is always roaming the halls ready to pull me into a room and make my toes curl.

He's especially bad when I come home from my soccer games. I'm irresistible to him when I'm all sweaty in my little shorts. He can't help himself. Last night I didn't even make it out of the entrance before he grabbed my ponytail, licked the sweat off my neck, then slid my panties to the side and fucked me from behind until I was seeing stars and screaming

out. Luckily, Evan was at his grandmother's house down the street.

What I also love about Carter is that he takes care of my mom as well. He always makes sure that her fridge is full of food and he's promised to make sure that the landlord is always paid. I always thank him profusely, but he just shrugs and says, "She made you and for that, I'll always be grateful." I mean come on, how cute is that? How could I not be in love with this guy?

Evan and I both scream as Carter rips open the closet door and roars at us like the big bad wolf that he is. My little hiding partner takes off running down the hall leaving a trail of giggles behind him and leaves me to face the big bad wolf on my own.

Carter's hungry eyes narrow on me when he sees me cowering on the floor of the closet.

"You don't run when you see a wolf, little bunny?" he asks in a husky voice as he approaches. I know what's about to happen when his voice gets all raspy like that and it's making my body tingle in anticipation.

"Not when the wolf eats me like you do," I say, spreading my legs for him. I pull up my skirt and show him that I'm not wearing any panties. The wolf lets out a low growl when he sees how wet I am.

As he comes down to take a taste of my honey, I jump up and run past him with a squeal. His hand shoots out and catches my wrist in a firm grip. "Not so fast," he growls as he pulls me back down. "You're not getting away from this big bad wolf."

I smile as he holds me down with his strong hand and spreads my legs with the other. Who knew that getting caught would be so much fun?

He reaches behind him and closes the door, plunging us into darkness. He wedges one of my new shoes into the door so we won't be interrupted.

It's pitch black in here. I can't see anything. I can just hear his heavy breaths and feel his strong hands keeping my legs spread apart.

My chest tightens with excitement and my pussy tingles as I wait for his hot mouth.

Suddenly, it's on me, hot and wet and messy and so fucking good.

My head drops back and my back arches as he buries his face in my wet pussy. He eats me out in a frenzy and I'm grinding on his mouth until I cum hard.

As my head spins and my body explodes in pleasure, I hear the clanking of a belt buckle and then quick and sudden, he thrusts his hard cock into me. He slides all the way in with one hard thrust and I dig my mouth into his shoulder to keep from screaming out.

He fucks me hard and fast. Urgency and need flow through his tight muscles as he drives his powerful hips into me one hard thrust after another. There's no soft love making and kisses this time. This is the big bad wolf consuming me, and I fucking love it.

If Carter could put more babies in me, he would. Unfortunately, we can only do one at a time, but that doesn't seem to stop him from trying.

His body tightens and he cums with a roar as he holds me tight. His warm cum fills me up and it feels so good that it pushes me over the edge as well. I hold onto his big muscular body as another orgasm slams into me and I spiral over the edge.

Luckily, Carter is there to catch me. He's always there to catch me.

It's one of the many reasons why I love him. One of the many reasons why I'm his.

EPILOGUE

Carter

Two Years Later…

The sight of Brooklyn walking around barefoot with her big belly sticking out does it to me every time. She just put the twins to bed and I just checked on Evan who is sound asleep. We have the house to ourselves and I got one thing on my mind.

She's eight months pregnant and the bottom of her belly is sticking out of her shirt as she walks past me with a seductive look on her face. Her tits are huge and my mouth waters when I picture taking one in my mouth and tasting her creamy milk.

"You look so beautiful with my child growing in you."

"Really?" she asks with a laugh. "Because I feel like a parade float."

"Come here," I say as I reach out to her, "and I'll show you how sexy you are."

Her tiny hand slides into mine and I pull her into my embrace. She grinds her sweet ass against my hard dick as I stand behind her, kissing her neck. My hands slide over her belly and then up to her big hard tits. We both moan as I run my hands over them.

Her nipples are long and hard and when I give them a little squeeze, a thin stream of milk trickles out and soaks through her shirt.

"This is all wet," I say as I grab her shirt and start to pull it up. "Better take it off."

She raises her arms as I slide her shirt off and toss it behind me. My hands are back on her bare tits and this time the milk gets my fingers wet.

"My shorts are all wet too," she says with a sly grin on her face. "Better take those off as well."

I turn her in my arms and drop down to a knee, bringing her shorts down along the way. She's gorgeous and I can't get enough of her.

Seeing her bred with my child always gets me rock hard. It's been one big love fest in here the past few months.

I reach up and take a few licks of her pussy as she holds my head with her trembling hands. Fucking her is so much better when I have the honey taste of her cunt on my lips.

I kiss my way up her round stomach and then lick her swollen tits, kissing and teasing each one before I get to her nipples. Her creamy milk leaks into my mouth as I slide a nipple between my lips and she moans as she holds my head to her chest for more.

I've never felt so lucky in all of my life. Ever since the night I first saw her, I've felt like the luckiest man on the planet.

I still have the souvenir that she left me of that night kept safely away in a fireproof safe. The sheets that have her first

orgasm on it are next to the sheets that have her busted cherry. After I took her virgin pussy for the first time, I stripped the bed bare and kept the sheets. I wasn't about to wash that off. It was too precious.

When I've had my fill of milk, I lay her on the floor and slide my hard cock inside her warm wet cunt. My seed is already planted in her womb and growing in her so this fuck is just for fun.

I can't wait until she has my baby and I can sink into her and put another child into her young ripe womb.

She bites her lip and moans as my cock drags against her sweet spot. Her entire pussy is *my* sweet spot.

We spend every night like this. Sometimes like tonight, it's in the kitchen, and sometimes it's in the bathroom or the bedroom or the living room, but every night I take what's mine.

And this pussy, this girl, is *mine*.

EPILOGUE

Brooklyn

Six Years Later…

"I can't believe it's been eight years already," I say as Carter drives down the highway. "It's flown by."

"Every second with you flies by," he says as he hits the gas, sending his new sports car rocketing down the highway. "If I'm not careful my life is going to flash before my eyes and I'll wake up in hell."

"Don't say that." I take his big hand in mine and run my fingertips over his knuckles.

"It'll be okay," he answers with a content look on his face as he turns to me. "I've lived in heaven since I first spotted you so it'll even itself out."

"You keep driving this fast and we'll both be there sooner rather than later."

He chuckles and then slows down. A bit.

"I'm excited to get to the hotel and rip that tight dress off your body."

"And then what?" I ask as I lean toward him, breathing in his rich smell. My pussy starts to get wet as he tells me what he has planned for it.

It's been eight years since I showed up at his doorstep as an eighteen-year-old kid to babysit Evan. Eight amazing years later and we're married with three additional children of our own.

Carter booked the penthouse suite in a gorgeous five-star hotel a few hours away to celebrate. We hired a babysitter to watch the four kids while we spend the weekend eating the best that room service has to offer off of each other's naked bodies.

"Then what?" I ask as he gives me the play-by-play.

"Then I'm going to bury my face in your dripping wet cunt," he says as his voice gets deeper and throatier, "and not come up for air until the concierge bangs on the door Sunday afternoon to tell us we're late for check-out."

"What about me?" I ask as I look down at the hard long cock that's throbbing against the inside of his pants. I lick my lips as I picture feeling it cumming in my mouth. "Doesn't my mouth get to have some fun?"

He looks over at me with a grin. "We'll see."

"Let's see now," I say as I drag my hand up his thigh. He lets out a low groan as I press my palm against his shaft and drag it along his thick length.

"We could do that," he answers in what sounds like one big long moan.

The car speeds up as I reach for his buckle and start to pull out his leather belt. My pulse starts racing and my mouth is already watering in anticipation as I reach in and pull his fat cock out.

My friends at school never understood why I went after

such an older man. Well, I don't understand why they didn't. Carter's cock is rock hard and I would bet he couldn't get this hard in his twenties.

I lick my lips and swallow the saliva in my mouth as I dip over the parking brake and open up wide.

Carter squeezes and twists his hands on the steering wheel as I slide him inside my mouth, dragging my cherry red lips along his thick shaft just the way he likes it.

I feel his powerful hand on the back of my head, guiding me up and down as I suck him off.

He's a good husband although he can be more than a little obsessed with me at times. I'm not allowed to talk to other men unless he's present and he needs to know where I am at all times, but it's worth it to have such a loving husband who makes sure that all of my needs are met beyond my wildest expectations. As long as I know that I'm his and act accordingly, everything goes smoothly.

"Shit, little one," he groans. "Your little mouth always treats me right."

I wrap my tongue around his shaft and drag it up to his head, sucking down the delicious drops of pre-cum that are oozing out of his dick. He grips the back of my head with a little more force as I dig my tongue into the little slit and try to get more of it out.

"Your greedy mouth never gets enough of my cum, does it?"

I can't answer with his cock in my mouth and I'm not about to take it out so I just keep sucking him harder, answering his question with my greedy tongue.

His foot hits the gas as I wrap my small fingers around his thick shaft and start jerking him off as I drag my tongue around the base of his head.

I can tell he's close to cumming. His massive chest is heaving up and down, his grip on the back of my head tight-

ens, and the car is swerving across the highway like he's a damn maniac.

I stroke him hard and suck even harder, urging him on with my little mouth.

"*Oh fuck!*" he shouts as he cums hard. I moan and cum too as hot spurts of his silky cream fill my mouth and drip out onto my cherry red lips.

I swallow him down and moan as I feel his warmth sliding down my throat.

This is going to be one hell of a weekend.

I lean back in my seat with a grin as I drag my finger along my lips, cleaning up the mess he made in my mouth. I suck the warm cum off my finger as he looks at me, shaking his head.

"I'm so happy you're mine."

I grin as I swallow him down.

I'm happy I'm his too.

The End

DON'T BE SHY. COME FOLLOW ME...

I WON'T BITE UNLESS YOU ASK ME TO

f facebook.com/OliviaTTurnerAuthor

instagram.com/authoroliviatturner

g goodreads.com/OliviaTTurner

a amazon.com/author/oliviatturner

BB bookbub.com/authors/olivia-t-turner

DADDY'S BEST FRIEND

BY OLIVIA T. TURNER

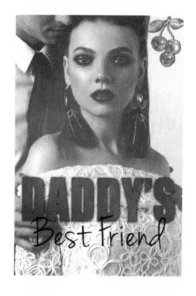

MY DAD **always thought of him as family. Would it be so bad if I made it official?**

I'm in love with my Father's Best Friend.

But as a nineteen-year-old virgin, I'm just a kid in his eyes.
At least that's what I thought…
When I get into some serious trouble, he's the only one I can call.
Logan saves me.
He's all that I ever wanted but this older man who I lust for has a secret.
He's Over The Top obsessed with me.
But I have a secret too…
I'm pregnant with his child.

CHAPTER ONE OF DADDY'S BEST FRIEND

Candice

"IS THIS REALLY NECESSARY?" I ask with my heart pounding.

"You've been arrested," the cop snaps back in a gruff voice. He squeezes my wrist a little too hard and yanks me forward. "Yes, it's necessary."

"It was an accident," I say as he opens the plastic case sitting on the table. It's a fingerprinting kit complete with the sponge that's stained with regrets.

The cop chuckles. "It's always an accident, or a misunderstanding, or a mistake. Finger."

He grabs my hand when I don't listen and pulls my index finger forward, nearly ripping it out of the socket.

"Ouch," I complain as he presses my fingertip onto the dark sponge. All of a sudden this is all feeling very real. I'm starting to get nauseous. *I hope I don't puke on the table.*

My finger is covered in black ink as he pulls it away and presses it onto my fresh new police file. He rolls it to each side and when he releases me, I'm the brand new owner of a criminal record.

"What happens now?" I ask as I try to wipe the ink off my finger and onto a Kleenex. It's not coming off. I've been branded a thief.

Too bad it's summertime and I can't wear gloves.

"Now you go to the holding cell," he says, closing my file. "Until someone comes to bail you out."

"Is that really necessary?" I ask again, getting desperate now. I can't call my Dad to come bail me out. He'll murder me. "I didn't mean to hurt him."

The cop chuckles again. "He's in the hospital right now getting stitches in his head. I would hate to see what you do when you're *trying* to hurt someone."

He deserves every painful stitch in his asshole head.

I exhale long and hard, trying to calm my swirling emotions. This is all happening too fast. I can't process it.

The cop brings me to a bare room with only a table, a chair, and a phone. It's one of those old, black rotary phones. I've never used one and I'm not sure if I even know how to.

"One phone call," he says.

I linger in the doorway, not wanting to come to terms with reality. Maybe if I stay here long enough he'll get bored and let me go.

Nope.

He pushes me into the room and grabs the door handle.

"Wait," I say, the word catching in my throat. "Who am I supposed to call?"

He shrugs. "Your parents?"

I shake my head. That's not an option. My strict military father would skin me alive and hang me from his mailbox as a warning to any other kids who considered breaking the law.

"Any other family?"

I shake my head again. Just my dictator of a dad and his bitch of a wife, my new stepmom. I'd rather rot away in a prison cell for all eternity before asking her for help.

"Lawyer?"

I shake my head again. My chin is starting to tremble. My eyes are burning. I want to go home.

"Then I don't know what to tell you," he says like he doesn't give a fuck. He slams the door closed, nearly making me jump out of my skin.

My heart is pounding as I walk over to the table and slip into the hard chair. I already know who I'm going to call but I just don't want to admit it.

I don't want him to see me like this. He already thinks that I'm a child. I don't want him to think that I'm a spoiled brat and a criminal delinquent too.

I pull the phone over and drag my fingertips over the cold metal as I think about him.

Logan.

Just the sound of his name sends warmth flooding through my body.

He's the reason why I'm in this shitty town. Brander, Colorado. I came for him.

Logan has been my crush for years. He's also my father's best friend.

My father, Brian, is a very strict military man. He was in Iraq when I was just a cluster of cells in my mother's stomach. One day, just after I was born, he was on patrol with his squad when they got ambushed. My dad was in the front and got shot in the leg as all hell broke loose around them. He went down and was immediately surrounded by three enemy insurgents who were dragging him back to be captured and tortured when Logan rushed out and saved him. My father never did tell me what Logan did to save his life. Whenever I asked, his face would go serious and he would get that distant look in his eye.

"It's not a story for children," he would always say in that condescending way that he still speaks to me in.

That's how Logan came into my family's lives. My Dad and he always kept in touch even though Logan lived in a

different state. We would see him on special occasions, some holidays, birthdays, stuff like that. Logan never had his own family so he kind of adopted ours.

I never really paid much attention to him until I saw him at my father's wedding. I hadn't seen him in over five years, since before I hit puberty, but I saw him then.

Holy shit, did I see him.

I was sixteen and a hot mess of hormones. My emotions and mood were all over the place but everything seemed to just click when I saw Logan walk into the church.

I still remember how my body shook when I first caught a glimpse of him. My heart was pounding in my tight chest as my breath quickened and my fingers ached with the need to touch him.

I can still remember every stunning detail. I've been picturing it every day since. He was wearing a dark gray fitted suit that is burned into my brain forever. His broad shoulders were making me lightheaded, his big arms making my mouth water.

"Hello, Candice," he said to me as he walked over. I was frozen to the spot, my pulse racing as he reached out his hand.

I gulped as I shook it, looking down as his sleeve rose up his thick forearm, showing off his sexy tattoos. I dragged my eyes up his muscular arms, to the red power tie that I just wanted to grab and yank toward me until his lips came crashing down on mine.

He looked just as shaken as I felt as he gazed down at me with his dark brown eyes that were brimming with something. I didn't recognize it at the time but now, looking back on it, I think it was desire.

Logan swallowed hard as he ran a hand over his strong jaw, while slowly looking me up and down. "You've...developed so nicely," he said, his voice low and grittier than I remembered.

A warm shiver cascaded through my body under his intense gaze. It was such a turn on to see an older man attracted to me, especially one as hot and off limits as Logan.

He was the best man at my father's wedding and I was the maid of honor even though I hated the bride and she hated me.

I always thought my father was strict until I met my stepmother. She is a real ball busting bitch.

Throughout the ceremony, I kept stealing glances at Logan as we stood across from each other. I saw him glance over at me a few times as he checked out my body and breasts, and every time it made me beam with pride.

I couldn't stop having dirty thoughts of him and I kept making plans throughout the rest of the ceremony on how to get him alone but it never panned out. I was too nervous.

He was a real man. Built like a truck and as sexy as a motorcycle. He wouldn't be interested in me.

Just when I was spiraling into a depressive funk, he asked me to dance and it was like my eyes were open for the first time.

He held me so close as we slow-danced. My nipples were painfully hard against his massive chest and all I could think about was losing my virginity to him. He was the only man that I've ever wanted and even now, I still hold my V-card. All because I haven't met anyone who could stack up against Logan.

"Hey!" the cop says, banging on the window and startling me out of my daydream. "You got one minute."

He gives me a nasty look before disappearing down the hall again.

I gulp as I pick up the phone, running my fingers over the rotary dial.

The last time that I saw Logan was two years ago when I was seventeen and leaving for University. All I wanted was to

be close to him so I picked a University that was twenty minutes away from his house.

I was thrilled when he showed up to my going away party and was over the moon when he offered to drive me back. I couldn't sleep or eat for days. I would be alone in the car with Logan for two hours. So many dirty thoughts raced through my mind and I wanted to make every single one of them come true.

But he wasn't interested. He was tight and awkward the entire time, like he was afraid to talk to me. It was only when he dropped me off at the dorms when we finally had the connection that I craved so much.

He scribbled down his phone number on a paper and placed it in my hand. "Candice," he said, cupping my hand with his two big palms. I felt so small as his powerful hands swallowed mine.

His dark eyes met mine and my mouth became moist as I pictured leaning in and kissing his soft lips. I could barely breathe in the car under his gaze like that. I would have gone anywhere with him at that moment. I would have done anything he asked.

"Here's my number," he said in his deep raspy voice that sent warm shivers flowing through me. "If you need anything. *Anything*. Call me. Day or night."

I needed something right then but I was too afraid to ask and unfortunately, he kept his pants on.

That was two years ago but I still have that number memorized. That paper is still under my pillow beside the picture that I stole from my Dad's photo album of Logan in his military uniform. I don't know how many times I touched myself while staring at it.

"Thirty seconds!" the cop says, banging on the window again.

I straighten up in my seat and start dialing.

There's a pain in my chest as I do what I've dreamed of

doing every night for the past two years: call Logan and ask him to come save me.

It's the middle of the night and after a few rings a groggy voice picks up the phone. "Hello."

I picture him lying naked in his bed, his hard beautiful body lit up by the rays of the moonlight drifting in through the window.

"Hi Logan," I say.

His heavy breathing stops.

"It's me."

Go to www.OliviaTTurner.com
to Keep Reading Daddy's Best Friend!

Made in the USA
Middletown, DE
05 June 2023